FOR MICHAEL

CIP Data is available.

First published in the United States 1994
by Dutton Children's Books, a division of Penguin Books USA Inc.
375 Hudson Street, New York, New York 10014
Originally published in Great Britain 1993 by Andersen Press Ltd.
Typography by Adrian Leichter
Printed in Italy
First American Edition
10 9 8 7 6 5 4 3 2 1
ISBN 0-525-45242-7

JEANNE WILLIS

IN SEARCH OF THE GIANT

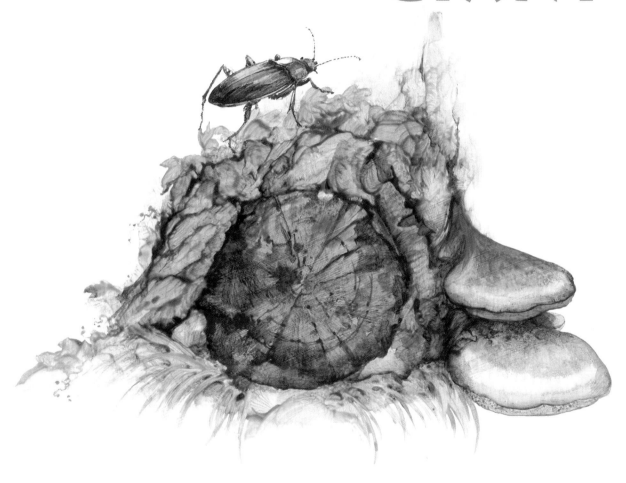

ILLUSTRATED BY **Ruth Brown**

Dutton Children's Books ◆ *New York*

Do you believe in giants? Did you say no? I thought so. There was a time, long ago, when I didn't believe either. But now I know better.

My older sister always believed. She told me story after story about the giant men who sleep for hundreds of years, until something wakes them.

One day she decided it was time for us to find a giant of our very own. There was a forest nearby where one might be sleeping, she said. Would I help her look for him?

Of course I had to go. How could I not? I
couldn't say I was scared—I didn't even believe
in giants.

We walked east across a field, then entered
the dark woods. We were looking for a creature
of enormous size, with a backbone as strong as a
beech tree, arms as long as elms, and thighs as
round as oaks.

Deeper into the woods we went, until we came
to a stream. Its banks steamed with moisture, the
scent rising thick in the air. Or was it the giant's
mossy breath we smelled?

We climbed up and away from the water, but
the smell lingered in the air like a magic cloud.
The butterflies and the squirrels seemed to be in
a trance. Perhaps they sensed tiny tremors in the
ground from the giant's breathing, heavy and
slow in his sleep.

A wind blew, and suddenly we were in his grip. Thorns caught and tore at my hair and clothes. Had we stumbled into a snare he had set for visitors who dared disturb him? I wanted to call out to my sister, but one look at her face and I knew she feared the same thing. Would we ever see sun or sky again?

At last we broke free. The tree branches seemed to beckon us on, but we felt as if we were walking around and around in circles. Soon the giant's scent began to fade. Perhaps we were too late. Maybe someone already had found the giant, and only his ghost was left.

Then we found another clue. A clump of his hair
was caught on a fallen tree. Hungry beetles and
squirrels rummaged through the tangled strands,
and a pair of wrens was building a nest
there. We hurried on, excited.

Animals often know things that humans don't,
like where to find a sleeping giant, or how to wake
him with a nibble. My sister almost hurried past,
but I noticed the fox kits, unafraid, gnawing on the
giant's fingertips with their tiny teeth.

What was that sound behind us? I heard a tree branch crack. Was he following us? Oh, no! Our careless steps had sent shudders down the giant's spine. He woke from his long sleep, stretching out his arms.

Stiff and sore, he raised his head. A giant
yawn escaped from his lips and scarlet
toadstool tongue, echoing through
the forest with an unearthly roar.

The forest floor shook as he rose to stand before us. Weeds covered his arms like a scarecrow's sleeves. His fists were scarred by the teeth marks of tiny animals; his fingernails were covered with fungi and moss. "Hurry and hide!" my sister screamed.

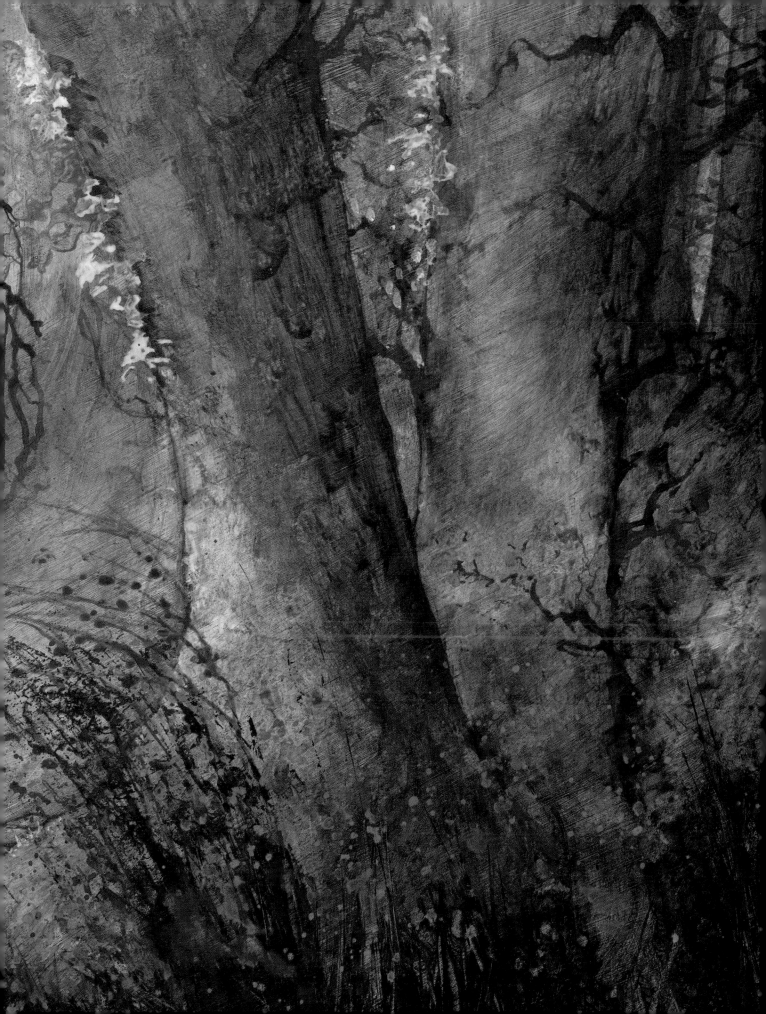

Was this what we had wanted? How could
we have known? I must admit we turned and
ran, as hard and as fast as we could. We ran to the
forest's edge, and then looked back. In the bright
sunlight, the trees behind us looked friendly and
inviting. A little sad, a little sorry, we wondered
if the giant's cry had really been a lonely greeting.
After all, even giants need company.

Perhaps you can visit a giant someday, near
your home. But I am sure of one thing—the less
we see, the more giant our imaginations grow.